THE FLUTE CONCERT

Wolf Harranth
Illustrated by
Romulus Candea

a **blackbirch** picturebook
woodbridge, connecticut

Published by Blackbirch Press, Inc.
260 Amity Road
Woodbridge, CT 06525

web site: www.blackbirch.com
email: staff@blackbirch.com

Originally published as *Das Flötenkonzert*
©1996 by Verlag Jungbrunnen
Vienna – Munich

©1998 by Blackbirch Press, Inc.
First Edition

Printed in Hong Kong

10 9 8 7 6 5 4 3 2 1

Library of Congress Cataloging-in-Publication Data

Harranth, Wolf
    [Flötenkonzert. English]
    The flute concert / Wolf Harranth; pictures by Romulus Candea.
        p.   cm.
    Summary: Having lost his sheet music, a flutist plays a concert from memory and
gives an inspired performance.
    ISBN 1-56711-803-8 (alk. paper)
    [1. Flute—Fiction. 2. Musicians—Fiction. 3. Concerts—Fiction. 4. Lost-and-found
possessions—Fiction.] I. Candea, Romulus, ill. II. Title.
PZ7.H2345F1   1998
[E]—dc21   97-38392
                                                                                                      CIP
                                                                                                       AC

Mr. August Winkelried was completely beside himself.
In just a few hours, he was scheduled to play the
famous flute concerto by Igor Klappenroth, in the great
Philharmonic Hall. But he had one big problem:
He couldn't find his sheet music anywhere!

"What's going on?"
asked Mrs. Hinklehopper, the housekeeper.
"I've lost my notes—my score!" August groaned.
"Your throat is sore?," asked Mrs. Hinklehopper,
who was a bit hard of hearing.
She offered him a cough drop.
"No!, not sore, *score*!" August exclaimed,
"I mean the notes I need to play the concerto!"
"Sorry, then I can't help you" said Mrs. Hinklehopper.
"But, I will go and warm up your supper."

August had no time for supper.
He searched everywhere for his notes—everywhere!—
but they were nowhere to be found.
August remembered that he had put his notes down
somewhere, nearby. But where?

As he searched, he found all kinds of other things
that had been missing for years . . .
a photo of old Aunt Caroline, his green silk
handkerchief, even the key to his favorite
wind-up clock.

As August wound up his clock, it began to tick
once again.
As soon as he had it set to the correct time, he stood
back to take a look.

"Oh, no!" he shrieked. "It's already seven o'clock!
Only half an hour before the concert is set to begin!
And I still haven't found my notes."

"What about supper?" asked Mrs. Hinklehopper.
"Forget my blasted supper!" August cried as he ran
frantically through the house, dripping with sweat.

The minutes ticked by.
August grew more and more worried.
By now, he was so upset that he felt like curling
up into a little ball and disappearing.

"What on earth should I do?" he wondered.

Often, when August had a problem, he would ask his niece Cornelia for advice. She lived in the same building, so finding her was easy. Timidly, August rang her bell and poured out his troubles to her.

"Have you ever played this piece before?" asked Cornelia.
"Not just once, but a hundred times!" answered August.
"And you still don't know it by heart?" Cornelia asked.
"Of course I know it by heart!" August replied.
"Then tonight, play it from memory, without your notes." Cornelia said confidently.
"Why, that's impossible" August responded, shocked at the suggestion.
"Anything is possible if you want it badly enough" said Cornelia. "And, I'll come along and hold your hand."

With his knees trembling, August shuffled off to the concert hall. One hand was being pulled by Cornelia. The other was free to wipe his sweating brow with his green silk handkerchief.

When August arrived inside the concert hall,
something strange happened. All his nervousness
simply disappeared.

"Where is your score?" asked the concert manager.
August craned his neck, puffed up his chest, and
spoke slowly:

"Tonight, for a change, I will play without the score.
Completely by heart."

"Why, that's impossible!" shrieked the concertmaster.

"No, clearly it is possible," replied August with a smile.
"Anything is possible if you want it badly enough."

At seven-thirty, the lights went down.
The concert began.
In the packed hall, some people sat coughing.
Those who weren't coughing were sneezing.
Those who weren't coughing or sneezing
were rustling their programs.
The people coughed, sneezed, and rustled right up
until the moment the famous
Concerto in D by Igor
Klappenroth began.

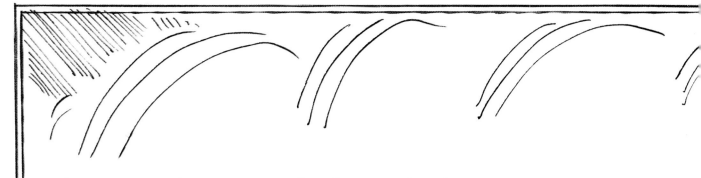

As soon as August put the flute to his lips
everyone became still.

August shut his eyes and began to play.
The music came forth from deep down inside him.
It flowed from August's lips.
It flowed from August's fingertips.
And, of course,
it flowed from August's heart.

August felt transported.
He floated on an invisible carpet of music.
He floated, weightless,
through a wonderland of extraordinary sound.

August's playing was so inspired that . . .
The conductor, being transfixed, kept his baton aloft.
This made the oboists turn bright red, holding their
note, as they waited for the baton to come down.
August played so beautifully that the bass player—
who usually seemed quite bored playing his
"shrumm-shrumm" back and forth—was filled with
the magic. This time his "shrumm-shrumm" quivered
like two butterflies in the Spring wind.

As soon as the last note sounded, August stepped off his "magic carpet" and opened his eyes. The audience exploded with applause.

Never before had anyone heard such a magnificent performance of the Klappenroth concerto. And no one, but no one, had ever played the concerto's three-part double trill in the second movement with such enchantment.

"Now you see!" whispered Cornelia, smiling proudly. "Anything is possible if you believe in yourself!"

Walking on a cloud, August returned home.

With a huge smile and a big hug, he said
goodbye to Cornelia and wished her
a good night's sleep.

After a few days, August found his score. It was in the bathroom under his shaving mirror. He had left it there on purpose to make sure that he would not forget it!
But, of course, that no longer mattered.

From that day on, he would play only by heart.